MEET THE
LINCOLN LIONS
BAND

OTHER YOUNG YEARLING BOOKS
BY PATRICIA REILLY GIFF YOU WILL ENJOY:

YEARLING BOOKS/YOUNG YEARLINGS/YEARLING CLASSICS are designed especially to entertain and enlighten young people. Patricia Reilly Giff, consultant to this series, received her bachelor's degree from Marymount College and a master's degree in history from St. John's University. She holds a Professional Diploma in Reading and a Doctorate of Humane Letters from Hofstra University. She was a teacher and reading consultant for many years, and is the author of numerous books for young readers.

MEET THE LINCOLN LIONS BAND

Patricia Reilly Giff

Illustrated by
Emily Arnold McCully

A YOUNG YEARLING BOOK

Published by
DELL PUBLISHING
a division of
Bantam Doubleday Dell Publishing Group, Inc.
666 Fifth Avenue
New York, New York 10103

ISBN 0-440-40516-5

Printed in the United States of America

October 1992

10   9   8   7   6   5   4   3   2   1

For my own dear Chrissie
with love

♪ CHAPTER 1 ♪

"**N**o talking, no noise," Chrissie Tripp whispered to Willie Roberts.

They crawled behind the hedge into Mrs. Niebling's backyard.

Mrs. Neibling had a great yard.

You could sneak through the bushes and climb the fence.

In two minutes you'd be in the Lincoln schoolyard.

Chrissie looked up. She could see to the top of the hill.

A college was up there. Her mother was in a classroom right now, studying to be a teacher.

Chrissie crawled faster.

She hoped her mother wasn't looking out a window.

It was September. The weeds were high and yellow.

Thankly, her cat, thought they were hunting.

She could feel his paw on her leg.

They *were* hunting, Chrissie thought. Sort of hunting.

Chrissie felt hot, sticky. She had to sneeze.

She held her nose together. One sneeze and Mrs. Niebling would be outside.

Chrissie clicked her teeth.

Mrs. Niebling would be outside in a minute anyway.

All because of Willie Roberts.

He was crashing along like an elephant.

"Will you be quiet!" She tried to keep her voice down.

Not down enough.

Mrs. Niebling popped her head out the back door.

Chrissie ducked her head.

So did Willie.

Thankly began to wash one ear.

"Out this minute," yelled Mrs. Niebling.

Chrissie looked at the schoolyard fence. One more second and they'd have been over.

They'd have seen the secret thing.

The thing that her older sister, Teresa, had been whispering about to Jessica Martinez.

"Out this minute," Mrs. Niebling shouted again.

Chrissie stood up.

She and Willie raced past Mrs. Niebling.

"Three more days until school starts," Mrs. Niebling said. "I can't wait."

Chrissie cut across Mrs. Niebling's lawn and out to the street.

"Yahoo," someone yelled.

It was Kenny Bender, skateboarding down the street on one foot.

That kid was always doing something dangerous.

"Car comes along, you're going to be peanut butter," Chrissie yelled.

"Do you ever mind your own business?" he asked, swerving to a stop.

Chrissie didn't answer. "Are you coming?" she asked Willie.

She headed for the corner.

She could hear Kenny on the skateboard. Talk about nosy.

She stopped at the schoolyard gate.

"It's too early to go in there," Willie said. He pointed to the sign.

SUMMER HOURS 10:00–5:00

Someone had painted an X over the sign.
Someone with black paint.
Willie's older brother.
Chrissie put her hands on her hips. "Teresa went in there, didn't she?"
"She's the school president," said Willie. "She can do anything."
Chrissie closed her eyes. All she heard about was her sister Teresa. Teresa can keep her room clean, make chocolate pudding, get A+ in everything. Her father always said Teresa was a doing kid.
Chrissie shoved the gate open and sped into the schoolyard.
She stopped to peek in the basement window at the cafeteria.
It was hard to kneel on the concrete.
She had a scab on her knee as big as an apple.

She could see no one was in there. She moved around to the doors and tiptoed in.

The school looked great. All the walls were painted yellow.

Willie's brother would be writing on them by Monday.

Chrissie started to run. She got up some speed and slid along the hall.

Then she stopped.

She could hear people talking in the music room.

It was her sister, big-mouth Teresa, and Jessica Martinez.

Someone else was talking too.

It was a man with a deep, rumbly voice.

"Drums," he said. "Fifes. Bugles."

Chrissie tiptoed closer.

Behind her, Willie and Kenny were sliding. Kenny was balancing his skateboard on his head with one hand.

She waved her arms at them.

Of course they were going to get caught.

"I hope I'm drum major," Jessica said.

Someone else spoke up. It sounded like the principal. "Professor Thurman," she said, "this is just what our school needs."

Kenny and Willie came up behind Chrissie.

"Stop breathing on me," she whispered.

She leaned back against the wall.

The Lincoln School was going to have a band.

Inside, a chair scraped back.

Chrissie gave Kenny a push.

They dashed down the hall and outside. Chrissie squinted at the bright sun.

"A band," Willie said. "Wow."

"I'm going to join right up," Chrissie said.

"Shoo," said Willie. "You can't play anything."

Chrissie put her hands on her hips. "I'll tell them I'm a drum player. Anyone can do that."

She marched toward the gate, head back, eyes closed. She played an invisible drum. "This old man . . . he played one . . ." she shouted at the top of her voice. "He played knicknack on my thumb . . ."

She crashed into someone.

"Oof," said a voice.

Chrissie reached out. She opened her eyes.

She was holding someone by the sleeve of a purple striped dress.

It was a woman so skinny she looked like a spider, one of those thousand-legger things that lived under the porch.

Chrissie stared up at her for a moment.

The woman looked as surprised as Chrissie felt.

Then Chrissie twirled around. She raced out the gate behind Willie and Kenny.

They didn't stop until they reached the corner.

"Who was that?" Willie asked.

Chrissie raised one shoulder in the air.

"Skin-ny," said Kenny.

Chrissie marched away from them and started for home.

She was going to have a pile of that left-over pizza—that is, if her brother, Joseph, hadn't finished it off.

A band, she thought.

What a year this would be.

She was always in some kind of mess.

But now she was going to be a star.

All she had to do was learn to play something. A drum. Something kindergarten simple.

And she'd be in.

Part of the Lincoln Lions Band.

She threw her shoulders back and swung her arms. "This old man . . ." she sang, "he played two . . ."

♪ CHAPTER 2 ♪

Today was the first day of school.

Chrissie pulled on her new red shirt with the gold stars.

It made her look like a band leader.

She marched toward the stairs.

She passed Joseph in the hall.

His hair was slicked to one side.

Joseph was a high-school football player.

Chrissie's father said he was the best.

Joseph was in love with a girl in his class.

Chrissie snorted.

Joseph was a mess. His face was broken out, and he looked as if he should shave.

The girl was probably a mess too.

Chrissie raced down the stairs.

Her mother had left already. She had an early morning class.

She had put everyone's cereal out.

A bowl of Cocoa Oats for big-mouth Teresa.

A bowl of Iron Man for Joseph.

And Honey Nips for Chrissie.

Chrissie poured her orange juice in the cereal. It tasted better than milk.

She didn't bother with a spoon. She drank right out of the bowl.

A couple of honey nips slipped out. They landed on the gold-star shirt.

So did the orange juice.

Chrissie brushed them off.

She could hear her father hammering outside.

She went to say good-bye.

He poked his head out from under a bench. "You look smashing."

Chrissie nodded. "Have to. I'm getting the best teacher in the school. Mrs. Monahan."

"That's lucky." He reached out. "Hand me that screwdriver next to your left hand."

She looked around. She could never remember that right and left business.

"Which hand is your writing hand?" her father asked.

She closed her eyes. "Left."

"Make believe you have a pencil."

She raised her arm and wrote in the air. "Got it," she said.

Her father smiled. "I always had trouble with that too."

She bent over for a kiss. "I'll try to remember."

Then she hurried to catch up with Willie

Roberts. Willie looked cleaner than he had all summer.

Except for his hands.

They had black paint all over them and a rim of dirt under his fingernails.

They turned in at the schoolyard gate and started for their line.

Willie grabbed her arm. "Shoo."

Chrissie stopped and stared. "Double shoo."

It was that skinny spider of a lady from the other day. Instead of a purple striped dress, she wore green . . . a hideous green that almost hurt your eyes.

Chrissie slid into the middle of the line.

She slammed into someone's ankle.

It was a new kid, with dark hair.

"Want a punch in the breadbasket?" he asked.

"Ex-cuuuuse me." She slipped into a spot behind Sarah Arlia.

"Where's Mrs. Monahan?" she asked Sarah.

Sarah raised one shoulder. "Having a baby, I guess."

Chrissie sighed. Her luck.

She looked at the rest of the class. No one else seemed to mind about Mrs. Monahan. They were talking, laughing, looking all polished up.

That idiot, Kenny Bender, was wearing a neon-orange tie.

The spider was counting. "Twenty-five." She nodded once and headed for the school steps like a racing giraffe.

The rest of the class raced behind her.

Chrissie took one last look outside.

Two birds were sitting high up on the telephone wires. One was singing.

Why not? He was free. He didn't have to spend the rest of his life in school.

Chrissie took a breath, then followed the class into Room 102.

Everyone dived for a seat.

Chrissie did too.

She was fast. Faster than everyone else.

She hopped over a chair and slid into a seat in the back.

The teacher's eyebrows shot to the ceiling. "Line up, everyone. We'll start over."

Everyone jumped out of the seats again and stood in front of the windows.

Chrissie bit at her lip.

If only she didn't have to sit up in front.

The teacher looked at them.

Everyone stopped wiggling.

The teacher spotted Chrissie. Her eyes opened a little wider.

Chrissie could tell she was remembering the other day.

"Try marching yourself up here to the front," she said.

Willie poked Chrissie, laughing.

She walked around the desks and up to the front.

Always a troublemaker seat.

She opened her new box of crayons and pulled out a sharp nile green one.

She drew a picture of the teacher . . . a spider body and a green dot face.

A moment later, the new boy, the fresh one from the line, banged into the seat next to her.

She saw him looking at her picture. She poked her nose into the air and sniffed.

She added a nile green spiderweb and the words "The teacher by C.T."

Then she watched Willie walk to a seat in the back.

Lucky Willie. He was so far back, no one would ever see him again.

Another new kid, a girl, sat on Chrissie's other side.

Chrissie took a peek at her while the teacher wrote on the board.

The girl had a terrible face.

She had pink glasses.

She smiled at Chrissie.

Chrissie blinked. She couldn't believe it.
The girl looked great when she smiled.
Chrissie smiled back.

The girl passed across a stick of gum.
The edge had been chewed off.
Chrissie could see teeth marks.

She closed her eyes and stuck it in her mouth.

The girl pointed to herself. "Michelle Swoop," she whispered.

"Christine Tripp," Chrissie said. "I'm the drummer in the school band we're going to have." She leaned over. "The band is a secret to everyone. But I got signed right up."

Michelle wrinkled her nose a little. "My brother used to play the drums. Made the world's worst racket."

"Fife," said Chrissie. "I meant to say I play the fife."

"Terrific," said Michelle.

The teacher finished writing.

MRS. LOLLIE LOVEJOY

She headed toward the back of the room.

She brushed past Chrissie, knocking the spider picture to the floor.

Before Chrissie could move, Mrs. Lovejoy swooped down and picked it up. She tossed it to her own desk in front.

Chrissie could feel her heart pounding.

It wouldn't take the teacher long to figure out who C.T. was.

She bit at the edge of her nail. Something else too. She wished she hadn't told Michelle that lie about the band.

She was getting to be a terrible liar.

♪ CHAPTER 3 ♪

It was Thursday. Ahmed, the smartest kid in the class, was putting multiplication answers on the board. Ten of them.

Chrissie hadn't even started math yet.

She was looking at her C.T. spider picture. It was still on the edge of Mrs. Lovejoy's desk. It lay in between a dish of paper clips and a dusty vase.

All Chrissie had to do was reach over and grab it.

Mrs. Lovejoy might never even know.

Chrissie didn't do it though.

She was sure she'd be caught.

Next to her the new boy, T. K. Meaney, was sneaking his lunch. It was pieces of thick, dark bread with raisins and butter.

Chrissie's mouth watered.

T.K. caught her looking at him.

He stuck out his tongue. It had a raisin on it.

Chrissie stuck her tongue out too.

He was the worst kid she had ever seen.

Eeeeekkkk went the speaker up in front.

"I know you're dying to work," said Mrs. Lovejoy from the back. "But let's listen."

Chrissie wrote one more number. Then she put her pencil down. She was sick of work. And next she had to read *People You Would Like to Know*.

Boringest people in the world.

They were all dead too.

Eeeeekkkk, went the speaker again.

"Good morning, Lincoln School," said a voice.

Big-mouth Teresa, Chrissie thought.

Teresa cleared her throat into the microphone.

Everyone jumped.

"Gross," said Willie from the back.

"Wonderful news," said Teresa.

Chrissie could tell that Teresa was nervous.

She was speaking fast, very fast.

Her voice went up and down.

"We're *having* a *school band,*" Teresa began. "It's *the* Lincoln *Lions* Band."

"Shoo," said Willie. "She's going a hundred miles an hour."

"We'll *go* to *parades.* We'll *play* for *parents.*"

Chrissie nodded at Michelle.

Michelle smiled back.

Michelle probably thought she knew everything about this school.

Michelle probably thought she was the world's best fifer.

Chrissie stared out the window. She half listened to Teresa.

Teresa was telling them that instruments were in the music room.

Teresa was saying that all they had to do was sign up . . . take music lessons after school . . . practice marching on Monday nights . . . and they'd all be great.

At the same time Chrissie was trying to figure how long it would take her to be the world's best fifer.

She sat up a little straighter. She'd do it.

Willie was already drumming.

She could hear him tapping on his desk with his ruler.

She stood up a little in her chair to see.

"Sign *right* up," said Teresa over the speaker box. "Fifth *grade* and higher."

Chrissie sat back. She couldn't believe it. Fifth grade.

She was out before she was in.

From the back of the room, Chrissie heard Willie. "Gonna take forever to get to fifth grade."

"Right," said Ahmed.

Kkkkk went the speaker.

Teresa was finished.

From the corner of her eye, Chrissie could feel Michelle's eyes on her.

She finished her math. Then she picked up her *People You Would Like to Know*.

She bent her head, staring down at the page.

Michelle leaned over. She gave Chrissie's arm a tap. "You said you were a fifer."

"I guess you didn't hear me right," Chrissie said.

Michelle narrowed her eyes. "I heard you say you played the fife and—"

"I do," said Chrissie. "I certainly do."

Michelle kept staring.

"I'm the mascot," Chrissie said. She put her finger over her lip. "Don't tell anyone."

"Lu-cky," said Michelle.

"Yes," said Chrissie. "Very."

Mrs. Lovejoy was staring straight at her.

Chrissie turned the page.

It was a new person.

She had zipped through about three without reading any of them.

How could she have said that to Michelle?

She took a quick look to see what Mrs. Lovejoy was doing.

Mrs. Lovejoy was writing on the blackboard.

She was still looking at Chrissie over her shoulder.

Chrissie started to move her lips as if she were reading. "Bla . . . blabla . . . blabla."

"Great book," Mrs. Lovejoy said. "*People You Would Like to Know*. I'll bet we know other people who are interesting too."

She tapped on the board with her chalk.

"Let's all choose someone we would have like to meet. Write and tell me why you would have liked him." She nodded. "By next week."

Chrissie rolled her eyes.

"Can't think, Chrissie?" Mrs. Lovejoy asked. "How about Sousa? Yes, John Philip Sousa would be perfect for you."

Chrissie sat up straighter. She started to ask, "Who . . ." Then she closed her mouth.

It was probably someone in the book.

She had doodled his last name on her book cover.

She couldn't worry about that right now.

The important thing was to get into the band. Somehow.

♪ CHAPTER 4 ♪

After lunch the next day, Chrissie stuck her hand up in the air. There was something she had to ask the professor.

"Yes?" Mrs. Lovejoy asked.

"I need to be excused for a drink."

Then she remembered.

Mrs. Lovejoy wasn't so hot on drinks.

"I mean . . . I have to give the house key to my sister, Teresa."

Another lie.

"March right on out," said Mrs. Lovejoy.

Chrissie marched out of the classroom.

T. K. Meaney was marching back in.

That kid is always out of the room, Chrissie thought.

She made believe she didn't see him. She looked down at the floor instead.

She took a fast slide.

Mrs. DiNardio, the principal, was coming toward her.

Luckily the stairs came first.

Chrissie slid along the banister for a few steps, then raced down the rest.

She slowed down when she neared the music room. Her mouth was dry.

The door was closed. She knocked, thinking about Mrs. Lovejoy. She had about two minutes to get back to the classroom.

She knocked again.

After a moment, she leaned against the door. She couldn't hear anything.

She looked up and down the hall, then turned the knob and went inside.

It was just the way Teresa had told them it was at dinner last night.

Teresa's class had their instruments.

Teresa wouldn't even let her touch her fife. "Go near it and you're finished," she had said.

Chrissie looked around. Musical instruments were all over the place.

Across the room were the drums.

Chrissie marched over and picked up a drumstick. "Bam de bam bam bam."

Easy as anything.

She could have been a star drummer in about two minutes.

She picked up another drumstick.

This one had a big lump on one end.

She pounded it into the bass drum.

It sounded terrific.

On the next table were a bunch of bugles. They were so shiny she could see her face in them.

She walked between the tables, stopping to pick up a blue-and-yellow pom-pom.

She gave it a couple of shakes, then wandered over to the table nearest the door.

A pile of fifes were spread across the top.

They were long, skinny, and a dark reddish color.

She picked one up. She'd just give it a little tootle.

She held it up to her mouth. "This old man . . ." she sang, wiggling her fingers over the holes in the fife. "He played . . ."

The door opened. Mrs. Lovejoy?

She spun around, heart pounding.

A man stood there. He looked older than Abraham Lincoln.

He had lots of gray hair.

He had a gray mustache too.

"I was just looking," she said.

The man smiled. "I'm Professor Thurman. That's a great song. Perfect."

He picked up a fife from his desk and began to play.

It sounded like the birds on the wire the other day.

It looked easy too.

All he was doing was blowing into one of the holes. He wiggled his fingers around on the others just the way she had.

Chrissie knew she could do it.

All she needed was a chance.

The professor played for another minute. "This old man came roll-ing home."

He stopped and nodded at her.

Chrissie smiled. "Sounds wonderful."

She swallowed. "Do you think you could use a mascot?"

"A mascot?" He drummed his fingers on the table. "Hmm. There's a band with a goat, and one with a donkey. I guess we could get a dog or a bird."

Chrissie shook her head. "I mean a girl."

"A girl?" The professor rubbed at his mustache. "Well, I don't—"

"I mean me."

"Why not be a fifer?"

"I'm not in fifth grade, not yet, not for . . ."

The professor frowned a little.

"I'd be good. . . ."

"I know you would," he said. He drummed on the table again. "Maybe . . ."

"A mascot," Chrissie breathed.

"I wasn't thinking of that," he said. "Maybe you could try out."

"Willie Roberts wants to be in it too."

"And that other one too," the professor said. He drummed faster. "Why not? Hard workers in. We'll let all the grades try. Start up a junior band."

"Great idea," said Chrissie. "Terrific."

"Remember, you have to try hard, and we'll see. If not . . ." He drew his finger across his neck. "Understand?"

Chrissie nodded. "Gonzo."

"Exactly." The professor smiled. "You have to know your right and left. You have to be able to march. Right face. Right flank."

Chrissie nodded. "Yes. Easy."

No, not easy, she told herself. She didn't know right, she didn't know left. She didn't know . . .

"Hup," said the professor.

Chrissie hupped out of the room.

She raced back upstairs.

So what if she didn't know right and left?

She'd learn the fife.

Kill two birds with one stone, as her mother always said.

She'd be in the band.

And Michelle Swoop would never find out what a liar she was.

♪ CHAPTER 5 ♩

"**J**ust let me try it," Chrissie asked Teresa. "I just have to . . ."

Teresa shook her head. "I don't want you slobbering all over my fife." She slammed her bedroom door shut.

Chrissie went down to her own bedroom.

She sat in her old chair next to the window. Outside, she could see Mrs. Niebling cutting the edge of her lawn with a scissors.

She could hear Teresa start to practice the fife.

"This old man . . . he . . ."

The fife made a terrible squeak.

Teresa had to be the worst fifer in the world.

If only Chrissie could get her hands on that fife for two minutes. She *had* to get her hands on it.

Michelle Swoop had called an hour ago.

She had invited Chrissie over tomorrow after school.

She said it was wonderful that Chrissie was so musical.

Just then the phone rang.

It rang again.

Chrissie could hear Joseph answer. "Teresa," he called. "It's for you."

Teresa kept playing. "He played knick-nack on my thumb."

"Teresa," Joseph screamed.

The fife stopped.

Chrissie could hear Teresa pounding down the hall.

Chrissie stood up so fast, she knocked over the chair.

She dashed down the hall on tiptoes to Teresa's room.

Downstairs, Teresa was laughing on the phone.

Chrissie picked up the fife from the dresser. She stood in front of the mirror and put it up to her mouth.

She did it just the way the professor had.

Get ready, she told herself.

She blew softly into the fife.

Nothing happened.

She leaned forward and tried again.

She knocked Teresa's birthday perfume over.

It spread across the top of the dresser, leaving a yellow mess all over Teresa's homework.

She rubbed at it with her sleeve.

It was sticky, very sticky.

Her nose tingled from the smell.

She heard footsteps.

Teresa was coming down the hall.

"What are you doing?" Teresa screeched. She grabbed for Chrissie.

Chrissie darted out of her way. She jumped up on the bed and down the other side.

She raced out of the room.

Teresa raced after her.

Chrissie tried for the front door. She didn't make it though.

Teresa spun her around by the sleeve. "I was saving that perfume—"

"You took mine last time," Chrissie said.

Teresa pinched her arm.

Chrissie pinched Teresa back.

A moment later they were rolling on the floor.

Teresa was older, but she wasn't a great fighter.

Chrissie was stronger.

She gave Teresa a punch.

Joseph stepped in between them. He pulled them apart. "Stop fighting, you two."

"Enough," their mother shouted from the kitchen.

Chrissie darted out the front door.

She raced around Thankly, across the lawn, and headed down the block.

She could feel a pain in her chest.

Maybe it was from the running, or because Teresa had socked her.

She didn't think so though.

It was because of the fife.

If she couldn't make a sound come out, she'd never get in the band.

She was going to be the same old Chrissie Tripp this year. She was caught between a doing sister and a football brother.

Michelle and Sarah Arlia would end up best friends.

She spotted Willie and Kenny Bender. They were skateboarding across the next street.

She called to them, but they didn't hear her. They just kept going.

She thought about going after them.

Instead she went back to her front steps, and listened at the door.

Teresa was talking on the phone again.

Chrissie went inside and upstairs to her bedroom.

♪ CHAPTER 6 ♩

It was Wednesday afternoon.

The class was cleaning out their desks.

Mrs. Lovejoy said they'd end the day with a clean slate, whatever that meant.

Chrissie pulled stuff out of her desk. A tennis ball. A homework paper with her footprint on it. Filthy. Half a pack of mints.

She leaned over toward Michelle to see if she wanted one.

Michelle shook her head no.

Chrissie didn't blame her. They were horrible.

The tennis ball rolled off the top of her desk and under T. K. Meaney's.

She reached for it.

Before she knew it, T.K. had the mints in his hand. "Thanks," he said.

Chrissie didn't answer. What nerve to take her candy. Even if it was the worst stuff she had ever tasted.

She looked up at Mrs. Lovejoy's desk.

She wondered if the teacher was going to clean hers too.

Chrissie could hardly see the spider picture. A box of chalk half covered it now.

Chrissie scratched at a stain on her shirt.

It was Teresa's second-best shirt.

This afternoon she was going to Michelle's house for the first time.

She took a breath.

She wouldn't even think about this band business.

She and Michelle would be best friends by the end of the afternoon.

Michelle wouldn't care one bit if she could play the fife, or the piano, or fly a jet plane to the moon.

Chrissie looked up toward the board.

There'd been a sign up all week.

PEOPLE DUE ON FRIDAY

She kept scratching at the stain.

Friday. The day after tomorrow.

Now, what was that all about?

The three o'clock bell rang.

"Ready?" Michelle asked.

"Ready," Chrissie said.

They went out the side door.

They talked all the way to Michelle's house.

Michelle had an older brother.

She didn't get into as much trouble as Chrissie, but she was terrible at math.

"I'm almost finished with Abraham Lincoln," Michelle said. "How's John Philip Sousa coming?"

Sousa? Where had Chrissie heard that? She wrinkled her forehead.

"My grandfather is always talking about John Philip Sousa."

Chrissie wondered what Michelle's grandfather had to do with Sousa.

She nodded as politely as she could.

They went up the front walk.

"I have a surprise for you," Michelle said.

A snack, Chrissie hoped. Maybe it was cake. Gooey. Chocolate, with those flat little nuts sprinkled on the edge.

"What kind of surprise?" she asked.

Michelle laughed. "It begins with an F."

F for Fritos? For fruit?

F for frankfurters?

Yes, frankfurters, she bet. She hoped Michelle's mother had piles of pickle relish.

Chrissie said hello to Mrs. Swoop and smiled.

Mrs. Swoop looked just like Michelle. Same long face. Same pink glasses.

She looked great, too, when she smiled.

"Come and have something to eat," she said.

The kitchen table was set with a yellow tablecloth. Yellow bowls and blue glasses were on each side.

"Butter pecan or peach ice cream?" asked Mrs. Swoop.

"Both," they said at once.

They had cookies, too, and juice. Chrissie kept thinking about the surprise. F. Ice cream? Cookies? No.

They went upstairs to Michelle's room.

"A little sloppy." Michelle looked embarrassed.

Chrissie started to laugh. "My room is worse."

Michelle opened her closet door. "I want to show you the surprise."

Michelle's closet was jam-packed. It had everything from hockey sticks to skateboards, books, and stuffed animals.

"It's here somewhere," she said.

She turned over a box. "Yes."

She held it up.

Chrissie felt her face get hot.

It was hard to swallow.

Michelle was holding a fife that looked just like Teresa's.

Michelle was smiling, nodding. "Play."

"Where did you get that?" Chrissie asked slowly.

"That's the surprise," Michelle said. "Listen."

She put the fife up to her lips. "This old man . . . he played one . . ."

Perfect. No squeak.

"My grandfather taught me," Michelle said. "He's the professor."

Chrissie swallowed again.

"We're just the same," Michelle said. "Isn't that something? I was so happy when I heard you were the band mascot."

Chrissie couldn't stop staring at the fife.

"Play," said Michelle. "Play anything."

Chrissie scrambled to her feet. She started for the door.

"What's the matter?" Michelle asked. "What's wrong?"

"Sick," said Chrissie. "Sick."

She rushed down the stairs, past Mrs. Swoop.

"Let me take you home," Mrs. Swoop was saying.

"No," Chrissie called back over her shoulder. "I'm all right."

She wasn't all right though.

She felt terrible.

She ran down the street, wishing she could keep running forever.

♪ CHAPTER 7 ♩

At three o'clock the next day Chrissie hurried down the stairs.

School was over for the day, at last.

What a horrible day!

Michelle had asked her a dozen times how she felt.

"Sick," she had answered. "Very sick."

And then there was that stuff on the blackboard:

MAKE SURE YOU HAVE WRITTEN
ABOUT YOUR PERSON.
DUE TOMORROW.

She couldn't even remember who her person was.

But right now she wasn't going to worry about that. And she wasn't going to think about Michelle, or the fife.

She had to be perfect.

This afternoon was the first marching practice.

She banged out the door to the schoolyard.

Piles of kids were hurrying out with her.

She could see T. K. Meaney had beaten them there.

He was standing next to the fence, holding the flag on a pole.

If only she had thought of that.

How easy to march around with a flag.

52

Just then the professor came to the door. He blew a silver whistle. "Line up, everyone."

Chrissie could see Teresa. She was wearing Joseph's football shirt.

She probably had on a ton of perfume. Joseph should give her a good punch.

"Eight to a line," the professor was saying. "Older kids in front. They're the seniors. Younger ones in back. The juniors."

Everyone raced around, trying to find a spot.

Chrissie could see Michelle in front of her. She ducked back next to Willie.

The professor blew his whistle again. "Is everybody ready?" he asked. "We're going to march. Right. Left. All over the schoolyard."

Chrissie looked at Willie. This was it.

She crossed her fingers. Near Michelle, Ahmed's fingers were crossed too.

"Forward march," the professor yelled.

Everyone in the schoolyard started to move.

Chrissie closed her eyes for a second.

She made believe she was writing.

Left.

She made a fist.

That way she could remember which was which.

"To the left . . . march," said the professor.

Everyone turned left.

Chrissie almost bumped into Willie.

She didn't though.

She didn't even have to keep her hand closed.

"Left right left right left right left," said the professor.

After a minute, everyone else was saying it too.

"Left right left right left right left."

Chrissie liked the sound of the marching on the pavement.

Left right left right . . .

Mrs. Lovejoy had come outside.

She was wearing a hot-pink dress with a ruffle on the bottom.

The ruffle was a little uneven.

It dipped up and down as she tapped one skinny foot in time to the marching.

Chrissie looked toward the front.

She could see Teresa swinging along in Joseph's shirt.

And there was T. K. Meaney, carrying the big flag.

Lucky.

She looked toward Michelle in front of her.

Then she looked toward the fence.

She could see Thankly parading along. He was looking at her too.

He had a smiley look on his face.

Chrissie smiled back at him.

"Left again," called the professor.

Chrissie took a nice big marching step. She turned.

She held her head up, her shoulders back as she swung her arms back and forth.

Then she realized.

Something was wrong.

Very wrong.

She seemed to be marching by herself.

Everyone had turned the other way.

She heard someone start to laugh.

She looked back over her shoulder.

Someone was pointing at her.

Chrissie just kept going. Across the schoolyard.

She saw the hot pink of Mrs. Lovejoy's dress in a blur.

She went out the gate.

Down the street.

All by herself.

♪ CHAPTER 8 ♩

Chrissie couldn't make up her mind.

Was it better to be the last one in school?

No one would have time to say anything to her—but everyone would look at her when she walked into the classroom.

She tied her sneaker laces.

Maybe it was better to be the first one in.

She'd go straight to the classroom, before anyone was even in the schoolyard.

She stopped in the kitchen.

She was starving.

She hadn't eaten a thing for dinner last night.

This morning Teresa had beaten her to the table. Her cheeks were puffed out with Cocoa Oats.

Teresa was excited.

The professor had made her the drum major.

Jessica could lead the juniors.

Chrissie didn't bother to sit.

She poured orange juice into her cereal. She jammed a pile of Honey Nips into her mouth.

Teresa was trying to talk.

Chrissie held up her spoon. "Don't say a word, Teresa."

She took three more enormous bites of her cereal and started for the door.

Teresa came after her, calling something.

Chrissie kept going down the path.

She knew what Teresa had said though. "I love you, Chrissie."

Chrissie swallowed. She looked back at Teresa standing at the screen door.

"I love you, too, Teesie." She started to run.

She was out of breath when she opened the classroom door.

She closed her eyes. She had forgotten her books, her lunch, and the paper.

The person paper she had worked on until bedtime.

She hadn't watched television.

She hadn't fooled around.

She had worked hard.

That is, after she had stopped sitting.

And she had sat for a long time . . . until it was almost dark . . . thinking about the mess she was in.

The band mess.

The fife mess.

The Michelle mess.

Then she remembered the sign on the blackboard.

Her person.

The name Sousa popped into her head. John Philip Sousa.

She hadn't done that.

She hadn't even started.

Another mess.

She got up and looked in the mirror. Even her hair was terrible.

She stared at herself.

Then she went downstairs for the scissors.

She cut bangs on top and chopped off about two inches in the back.

It was uneven.

But she looked a little different, a little better.

She got out the people book.

There was John Philip Sousa, right on page twenty.

She sat down and read slowly.

Mrs. Lovejoy was right.

He was a person Chrissie would like to have known.

He was a band person.

And she could see why Mrs. Lovejoy had told her about him.

She couldn't believe her paper was home. Home on the table.

She walked into the classroom.

She sat down in her seat.

Behind her there was a noise.

She jumped.

It was Mrs. Lovejoy, snapping up a shade.

"I didn't know you were here." Chrissie could feel her cheeks getting hot.

Mrs. Lovejoy came to the front.

Chrissie sighed. "I forgot my person paper at home."

"Your hair, Chrissie." Mrs. Lovejoy turned her head to one side. "It looks . . ."

Chrissie ran her hand over the top of her head. "My mother said she liked it."

Mrs. Lovejoy thought about it for a moment. "I like it too," she said.

"About the paper," Chrissie said. "I did it, really. I wrote about how he loved to march . . . how he wrote music for bands. . . ."

"I saw you marching yesterday," Mrs. Lovejoy said.

Chrissie ducked her head. "I liked him, too, because he was going to run away. He was going to join the circus."

"I wanted to join the circus," said Mrs. Lovejoy. "I was always sloppy. Always in trouble."

Her face looked soft.

She didn't look one bit like a spider.

Chrissie looked at the desk.

She didn't see the spider picture.

It would be terrible if Mrs. Lovejoy had seen it.

Terrible.

"You're a great marcher," Mrs. Lovejoy said. "I thought that the first time I saw you."

"I'm a terrible marcher."

Mrs. Lovejoy smiled. "Not so hot with the rights and the lefts, but you can fix that."

Chrisie shook her head again. "I'm not in the band anyway."

Mrs. Lovejoy leaned forward. "I think you're going to be surprised," she said. "In the meantime, don't forget to bring me Sousa on Monday." She smiled. "And how about pulling up that last shade for me?"

Chrissie went over to the window.

She could see Michelle coming across the schoolyard.

She wished she knew where a circus was.

She'd run away before the bell rang.

♪ CHAPTER 9 ♩

Five minutes later the classroom was full.

Chrissie didn't look up.

Out of the corner of her eye, she could see Michelle's seat was still empty.

She wondered why it was taking Michelle so long to get into the classroom.

T. K. Meaney slid into the seat on her other side.

He leaned over.

He dropped a crumpled-up piece of paper on her desk.

Chrissie stared at it for a moment.

Then her fingers closed around it.

She didn't have to open it to know it was the spider picture.

She looked over at T.K.

"For the mints," he said.

She nodded a little, thinking.

T.K. was going to be her friend, she knew it.

She walked up to the wastebasket.

She stood there a minute, carefully tearing the paper into small pieces.

Maybe Mrs. Lovejoy had never seen the spider picture.

Chrissie hoped not.

She couldn't even imagine why she thought Mrs. Lovejoy had looked like a spider.

She went back to her seat.

Eeeeekkkk went the loudspeaker.

A rumbling voice came on. "Good morning, Lincoln School."

It was the professor.

"Wonderful news," he said. "Our senior band looks good. Our junior band too. Everyone is in."

He cleared his throat. "I have a special thank you," he said. "It's to Christine Tripp. She's the one who picked our marching song."

Chrissie looked down at her desk.

Her eyes stung.

"Listen to Michelle . . ." the professor was saying.

A moment later came the sound of a fife.

Michelle's fife.

She was playing "This old man . . . he played one . . ."

Up in front of the room, Mrs. Lovejoy was clicking skinny fingers to the music.

T.K. was tapping his feet.

And in back somewhere, Willie was drumming on his desk with something.

Probably his people book.

John Philip Sousa would have loved it.

Chrissie loved it.

She was going to be in the band. Maybe not a star.

But in.

Just then, the song ended. "With a knick-knack paddy wack, give the dog a bone . . ."

Everyone in the class finished, singing, "This old man came rolling home."

"And now," said the professor, "it's time for the junior fifers. Come down for your first lesson."

For a moment, Chrissie sat there.

She watched Ahmed and Sarah Arlia go out the door.

Then Mrs. Lovejoy smiled at her. "I told you," she said.

Chrissie stood and followed them down the hall.

She was going to learn her left from her right.

Today.

She was going to learn the fife.

Maybe not today, but soon.

And she was going to tell Michelle the truth.

She was going to say that she had never even seen a fife before school started.

She was going to say she was never a mascot, never in a band.

But there was something else.

She was going to say that she loved to march and she was going to learn to play the fife.

Michelle was waiting at the music room door for her.

Chrissie ran to catch up.

"Hey, Michelle . . ." she began.

It was going to be a wonderful year.

She couldn't wait for the first parade.